Geoffrey Patterson was an interior designer and a set designer for the BBC, before becoming an author and illustrator of children's books. His previous titles for Frances Lincoln are *Indigo and the Whale*, written by Joyce Dunbar, *The Lion and the Gypsy*, which was nominated for the Kate Greenaway Medal, and *Stories from the Bible*, written by Martin Waddell.
Geoffrey divides his time between Norwich and the South of France.

JONAH
AND THE
WHALE

GEOFFREY PATTERSON

FRANCES LINCOLN

Jonah lived in a small village, in the land of Israel.
He was a lazy man, who spent most of the day lying in
the sun doing nothing, while his neighbours worked hard.

The people in the village kept away from Jonah because he was so lazy. This made Jonah unhappy, and at last he asked himself why he found it so difficult to be like them.

Then Jonah heard the voice of God.

"Get up!" said God. He told Jonah to go to the great city of Nineveh and make the people stop their endless fighting with the people of Israel.

But Jonah said to himself, "I can't possibly do that. I am just an ordinary man. Perhaps the people of Nineveh will kill me. I won't go!"

Again he heard the voice of God: "Jonah, you *must* go. I have chosen you."

By now Jonah was so frightened that he decided to run away.

Early the next day he went to the little port
of Joppa. There he boarded a wooden cargo boat
bound for Tarshish, far away from
Israel and Nineveh.

The boat set sail, and soon they were out of sight of land.
Jonah hoped he was out of sight of God, too.

The days and nights passed.

Late one evening the weather grew suddenly stormy.
The sea became dark, inky black, the waves rose
higher and higher, and the sky turned grey,
the colour of granite. The ship was violently
tossed about, tipping the cargo overboard.

Everyone on the boat was afraid and prayed to their Gods
to save them from the storm. All except Jonah. He was
fast asleep in the ship's hold.

The others woke him up. "How can you sleep in such
a terrible storm?" they cried. "Who are you?
Why are you here?"

Then Jonah realised that God had made the storm because
he had tried to run away.

"The only way to save yourselves is to throw me into the sea," he said. "Then God will stop the storm."

So reluctantly they took Jonah and threw him over the side into the raging sea.

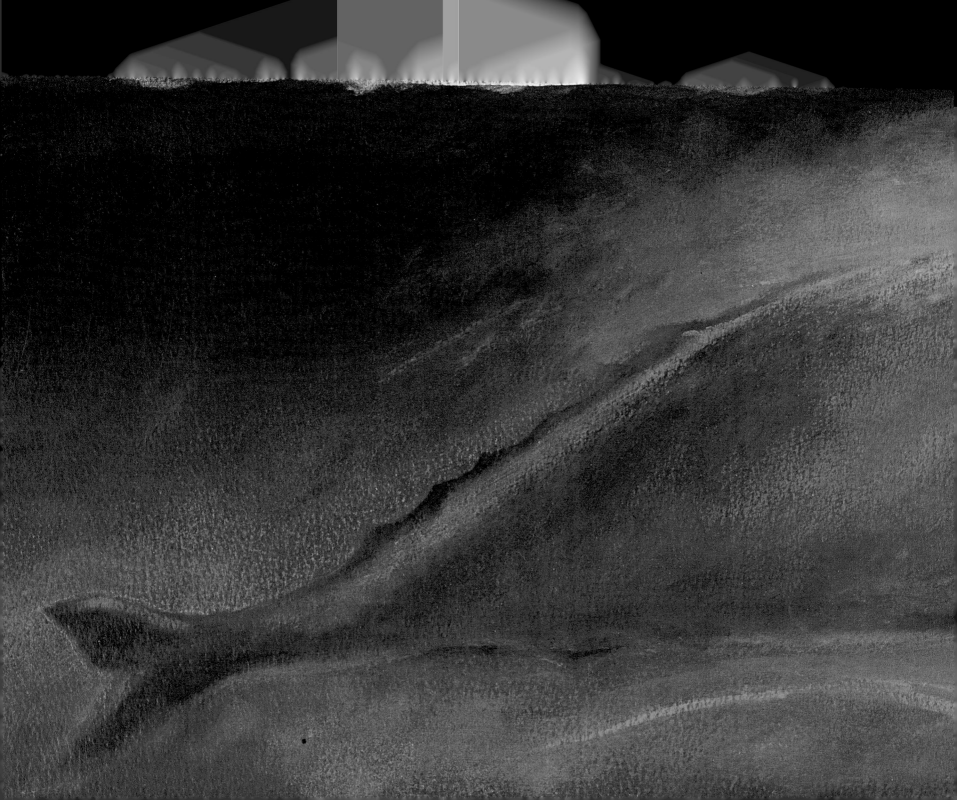

Instantly the sea became calm.
But Jonah sank slowly down and down, into the darkness. Surely he would drown.

Then out of the blue-black depths appeared an enormous whale many times the size of the ship. With one gulp, it swallowed up little Jonah.

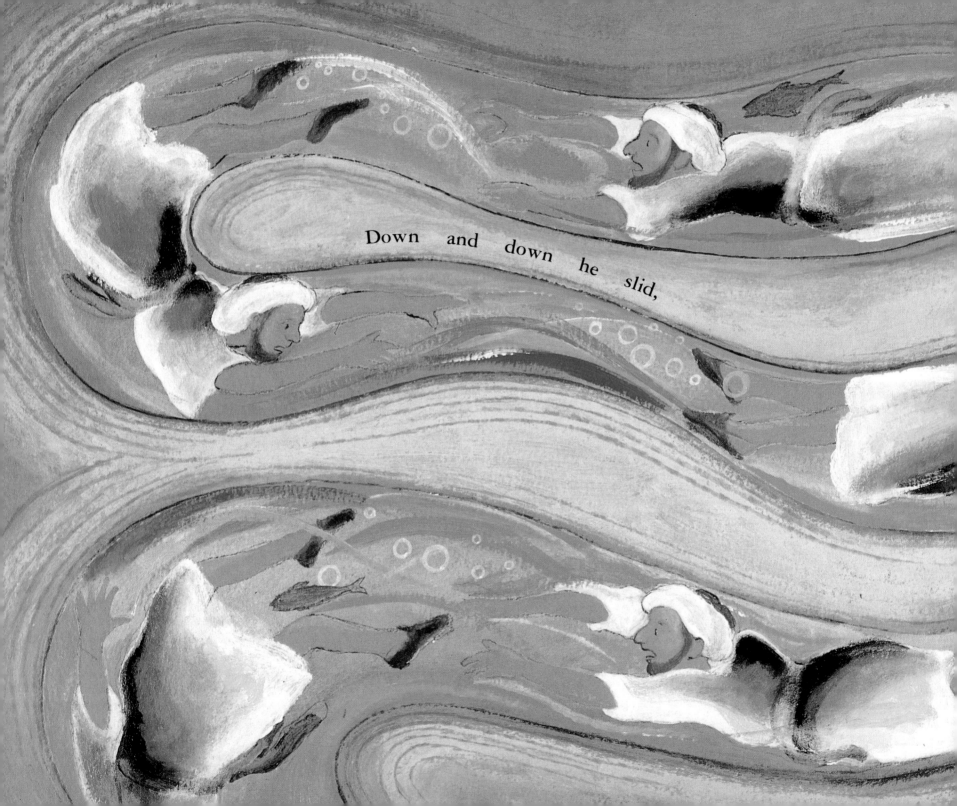

Down and down he slid,

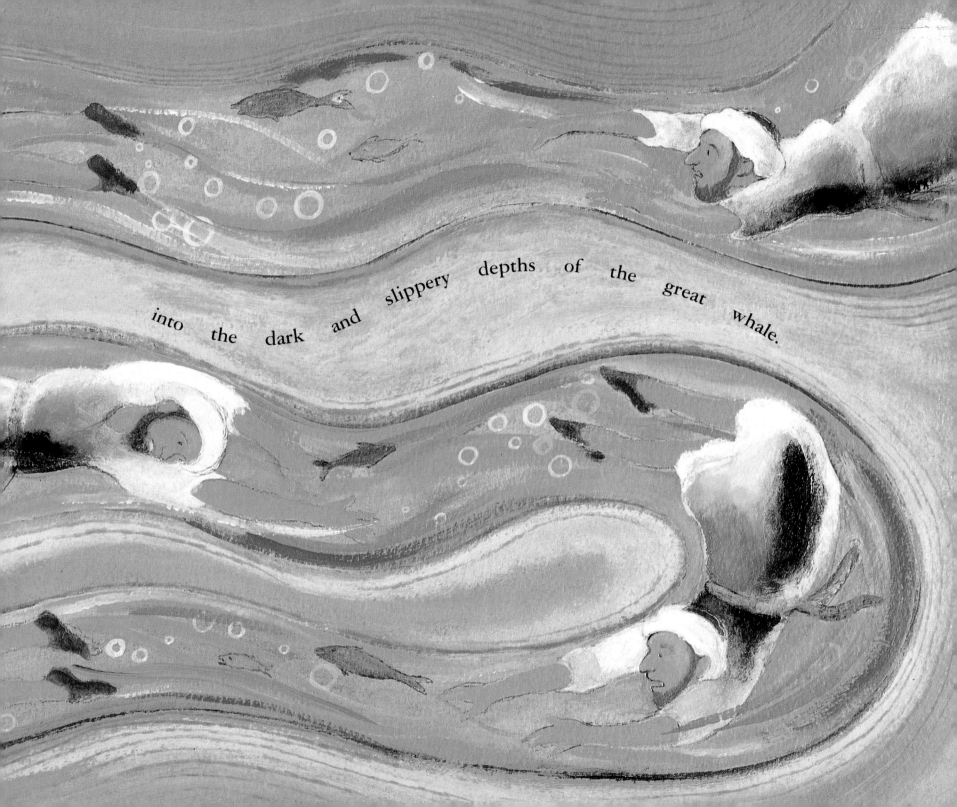

into the dark and slippery depths of the great whale.

At last he came to a stop in the whale's stomach.

It was dark and damp and strange rumbling noises echoed around him.
Poor Jonah sat huddled up for many hours, feeling very sorry for himself.
But then he realised that the whale had saved him from drowning, and he
began to understand that he was inside the whale because he had tried
to run away from God.

Jonah spoke to God from the whale's stomach and said: "I trust you
to look after me, and I will do what you ask."

At that moment a light began to glow inside the giant cavern of the
whale's stomach, and Jonah could look around.

For three days and three nights the mighty whale
plunged through the ocean.

On the morning of the fourth day, Jonah felt
the inside of the whale heave and shake like an earthquake.
   Jonah was terrified. "What's happening?" he cried.
   Then he was thrown up in the air, and with a gurgle and
a whoosh he was pushed and squeezed along a dark slippery tunnel.

Suddenly he saw daylight. The whale's great mouth had opened.

A moment later Jonah was spewed out of the whale and on to the shore!

He knelt beside the sea, raised his hands to God and thanked Him for saving his life. "Now I will go to Nineveh and give them your message," he said.

The great whale looked at Jonah for a long moment, and then it slowly sank back into the sea.

For Bonny

MORE PICTURE BOOKS IN PAPERBACK
FROM FRANCES LINCOLN

INDIGO AND THE WHALE
Geoffrey Patterson

The spellbinding story of Indigo, who charms a whale with his pipe-playing
and finds himself on a momentous journey of discovery.

Suitable for National Curriculum English – Reading, Key Stages 1 and 2
Scottish Guidelines English Language – Reading, Level B

ISBN 0-7112-1080-2 £4.99

STORIES FROM THE BIBLE
Martin Waddell
Illustrated by Geoffrey Patterson

Seventeen lively stories retold from the Scriptures in language children
everywhere will enjoy – a perfect introduction to the Old Testament.

Suitable for National Curriculum English – Reading, Key Stage 2; Religious Education, Key Stage 2
Scottish Guidelines English Language – Reading, Levels B and C; Religious and Moral Education, Levels B and C

ISBN 0-7112-1845-5 £6.99

KASPAR'S GREATEST DISCOVERY
Campbell Paget
Illustrated by Reg Cartwright

Through the amusing story of Kaspar the astronomer,
Campbell Paget retells the much-loved tale of the Three Wise Men.

Suitable for National Curriculum English – Reading, Key Stages 1 and 2; Religious Education, Key Stages 1 and 2
Scottish Guidelines English Language – Reading, Levels B and C; Religious and Moral Education, Levels B and C

ISBN 0-7112-1174-4 £4.99

Frances Lincoln titles are available from all good bookshops.
Prices are correct at time of publication, but may be subject to change.